FLASH MAX
Fire Safety Superhero

To my children Madison, Mason and Jocelyn,

who inspired me to create the Flash Max character.

Daddy loves you!

Text Copyright © 2016 by Michael Furman
Illustration Copyright © 2016 by Michael Furman

First edition 2016

Published in the United States by Pfun-omenal Stories LLC,
Deer Park, New York

Designed by Todd Lape / Lape Designs

www.PfunomenalStories.com

Printed in the United States by Phoenix Color

ISBN-13: 978-0-9906494-3-4

About the Author/Illustrator

Michael Furman is a 16 year veteran professional
firefighter with the Fairfax County Fire and Rescue
Department in Virginia assigned to Truck Company 411
at the Penn Daw Firehouse, where he currently holds
the rank of Master Technician (Driver / Operator).

He is a 30 year life member of the LaPlata Volunteer
Fire Department in Charles County, Maryland, where
he resides with his wife Heidi. and three children,
as well as a veteran of the United States Air Force,
having served as a Firefighter and Rescue Specialist
at Nellis Air Force Base in Nevada from 1989 to 1992.

Meet my sidekick Al-Arm,
the Smoke Alarm.

Al-Arm is always standing guard for
you—watching and smelling for smoke—
even while you're sleeping at home!

Al-Arm and I can't do this alone.

We need YOUR help, too.

You can help in the fight to keep
us all safe from fires. . .

Home fire prevention awareness began many years ago, after the Great Chicago Fire of 1871, which started accidentally and burned for days. Many homes, buildings, and lives were lost.

Americans observe Fire Prevention
Week every year during the week of
October 9th, the anniversary
of that Great Chicago Fire.

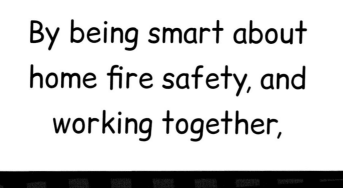

By being smart about home fire safety, and working together,

we can beat Blaze by knowing what
to do if he ever shows up!

Did you know that you and your family have very important jobs in helping me and Al-Arm in the fight against Blaze?

You do!

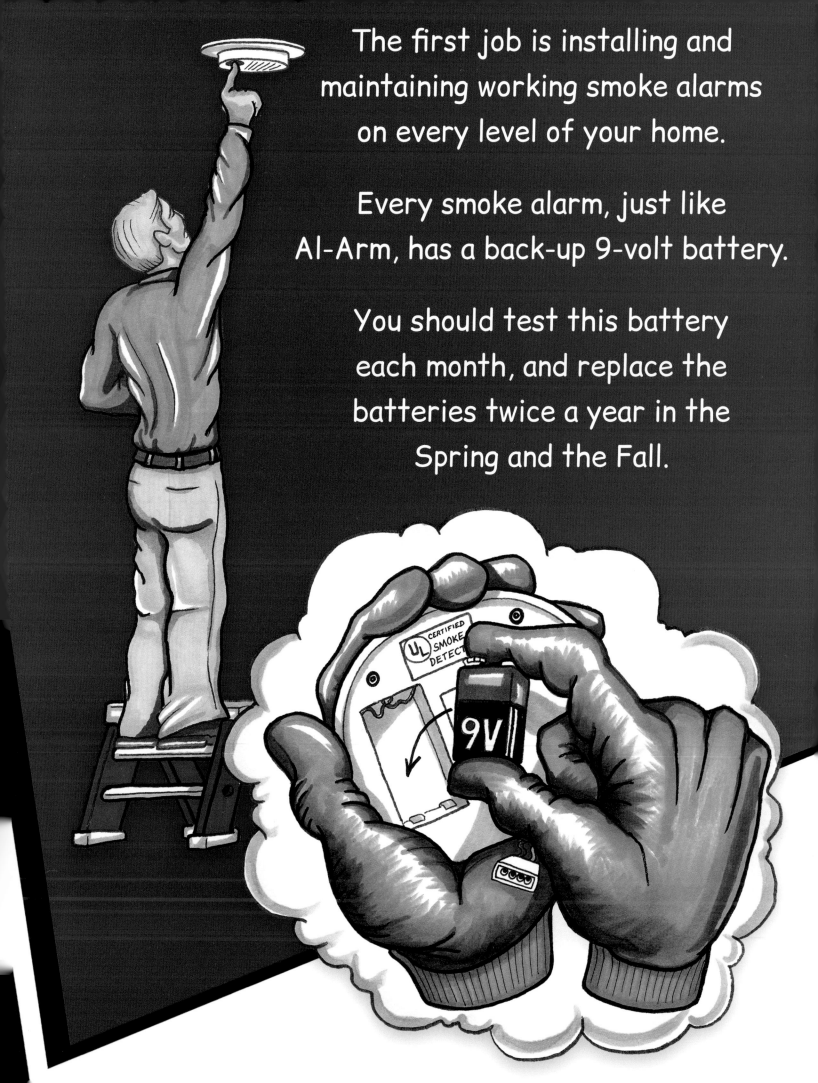

The first job is installing and maintaining working smoke alarms on every level of your home.

Every smoke alarm, just like Al-Arm, has a back-up 9-volt battery.

You should test this battery each month, and replace the batteries twice a year in the Spring and the Fall.

Testing your smoke alarms is easy.
Have your parents or an adult
simply press and hold the 'TEST'
button until the alarm sounds.

This is the same sound you would hear if your smoke alarm, just like Al-Arm, detects smoke in your home, meaning Blaze could be nearby!

You must act quickly!

Which brings us to your next
and equally important home
fire safety job—developing and
practicing a family home fire escape plan together.

Families who are prepared with an escape
plan know how to stay low and go!

Heat and smoke rise, so crawl low
where there is less smoke.

Do you sleep with your bedroom
door closed at night? Well you should!

Meet our other friend, Zoor the Door!

Your door, like Zoor, acts like a
security guard against smoke and Blaze,
giving you extra time to escape.

If you hear your smoke alarm going off at night, crawl out of bed over to your bedroom door and feel it with the back of your hand. If it feels hot, do not open it, because Blaze could be on the other side!

Have a second way out!
If your bedroom door was hot,
how would you escape?
Remember, do not hide, go outside!
To get help, open your bedroom window and signal for help.

You'll want to get out and stay out!
Everyone in your family should go to a
special meeting place and stay there.
Remember, never, ever, go back
inside for any reason!

Someone in the family needs to call
the emergency number from the outside
of the home with the fire.
Tell the emergency operator your name,
address, and type of emergency.
Then wait outside until the firefighters arrive.
Don't worry, they are on their way!

Stay at your family's meeting place until the firefighters arrive. When they do, one of the adults should tell the firefighters if everyone in your family got out safely.

Finally, what would you do if
your clothes were on fire?
Stop, drop, and roll!
Rolling on the ground helps to smother
the flames and put the fire out.

Did you know we get our special
superhero powers from all of you?
Every time you practice fire safety skills,
Flash Max and Al-Arm get stronger!
It's been fun learning about fire safety together today.
Until next time, friends,
BE SMART, HAVE A PLAN, and STAY LOW!